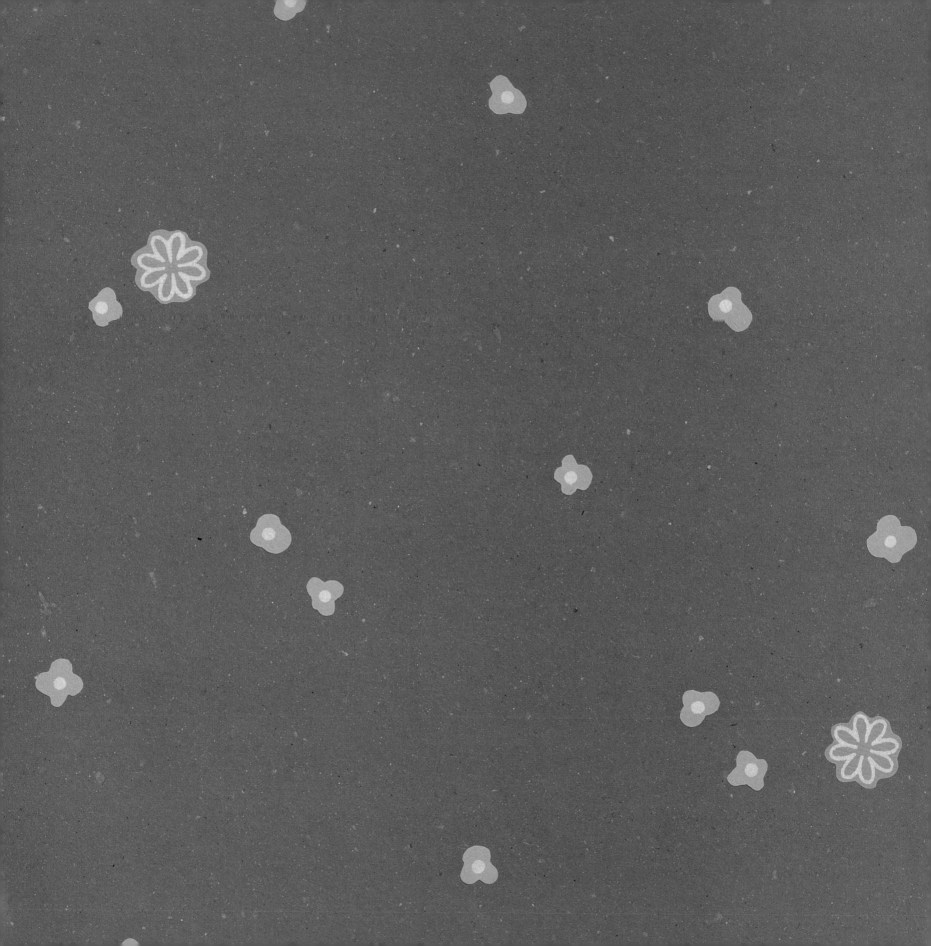

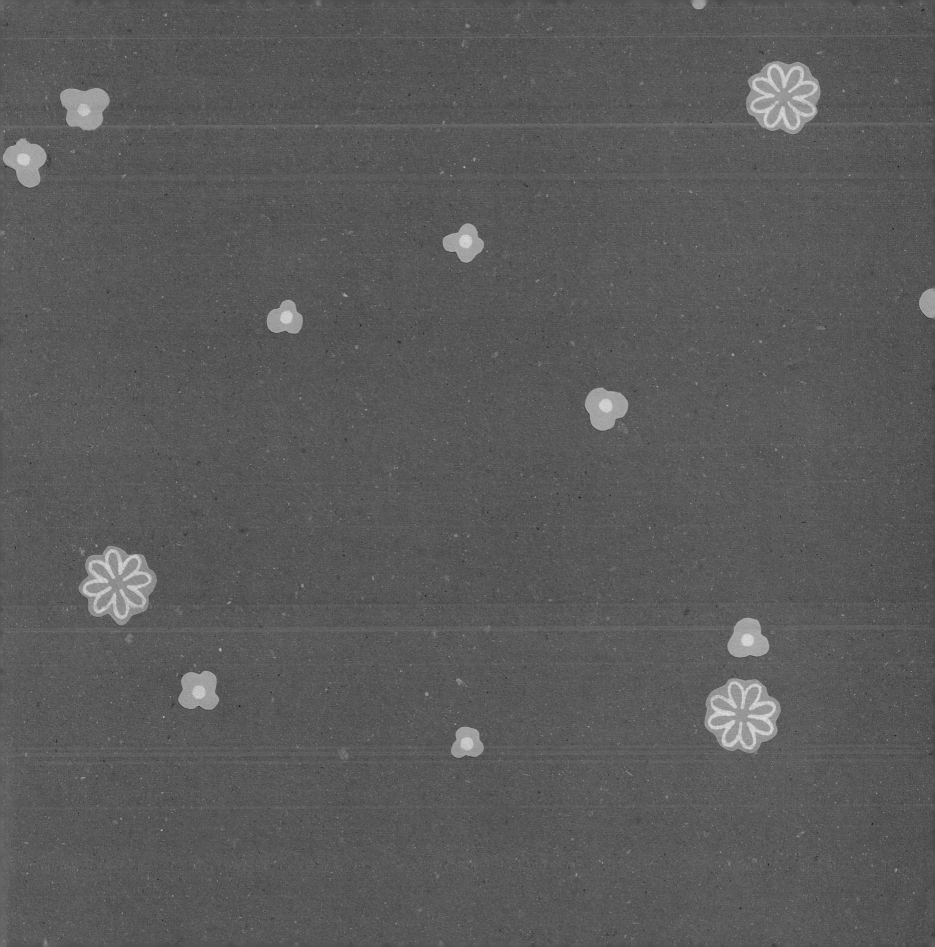

For Meg & Lucy,
Eunice's four-legged friends! ~ CJC

SIMON AND SCHUSTER

First published in Great Britain in 2007 by Simon & Schuster UK Ltd
Africa House, 64-78 Kingsway, London WC2B 6AH
A CBS COMPANY

This paperback edition first published in 2007

Book design by Genevieve Webster
The text for this book is set in Hank
The illustrations are rendered in mixed media

A CIP catalogue record for this book is available from
the British Library upon request

ISBN 978 1 41690 402 1

Printed in China
3 5 7 9 10 8 6 4 2

Come On, Digby!

Caroline Jayne Church

SIMON AND SCHUSTER
London New York Sydney

On the farm lived two cows, four pigs,
six silly sheep and a grumpy farmer.

There was also a new sheepdog, called Digby.

Digby had been brought to the farm because he
was so very good at herding sheep.

"Right, Digby," said the farmer.
"Let's see just how good you really are.
I want all those sheep
in the pen, now!"

"Easy-peasy!" thought Digby.
"Only six sheep!"

So he set to work.

But these sheep had different ideas.

They didn't like being told where to go, or what to do.

This made Digby cross. He pulled a ferocious face and growled at them.

But the sheep shrugged and wandered off
to eat some tasty grass.

Digby was furious, and confused.

How could he possibly be a great sheepdog
if the sheep completely ignored him?

So he came up with a plan...

"Into the pen, NOW!" he yelled over the noise of the engine.

But the sheep just smiled.

Digby had another idea.

"Into the pen, NOW!" he shouted
over the roar of the tank.

But the sheep weren't scared.

So he took to the skies in a huge helicopter.

"Into that pen, NOW!"

Digby cried at the top of his voice.

But the sheep simply looked up and laughed.

Digby felt exhausted. He didn't know what to do next.
"How can I be a great sheepdog if I can't even
round up six silly sheep?"

He hung his head in misery.

The two cows and four pigs saw how unhappy he was.
"Come on, Digby!" they said, encouragingly.
"We have lived on this farm for a long time,"
they told him. "And we've learnt there is a way
to get what we want!"

They gathered round Digby, and whispered their secret.

"Why, thank you!" said Digby. "Now I think I understand."

He took a deep breath and wandered over
to the sheep.
"Would you go into your pen now... please?"

One by one, the sheep went quietly into the pen.
And Digby never had any trouble with the
sheep again.

But the ducks were another matter...

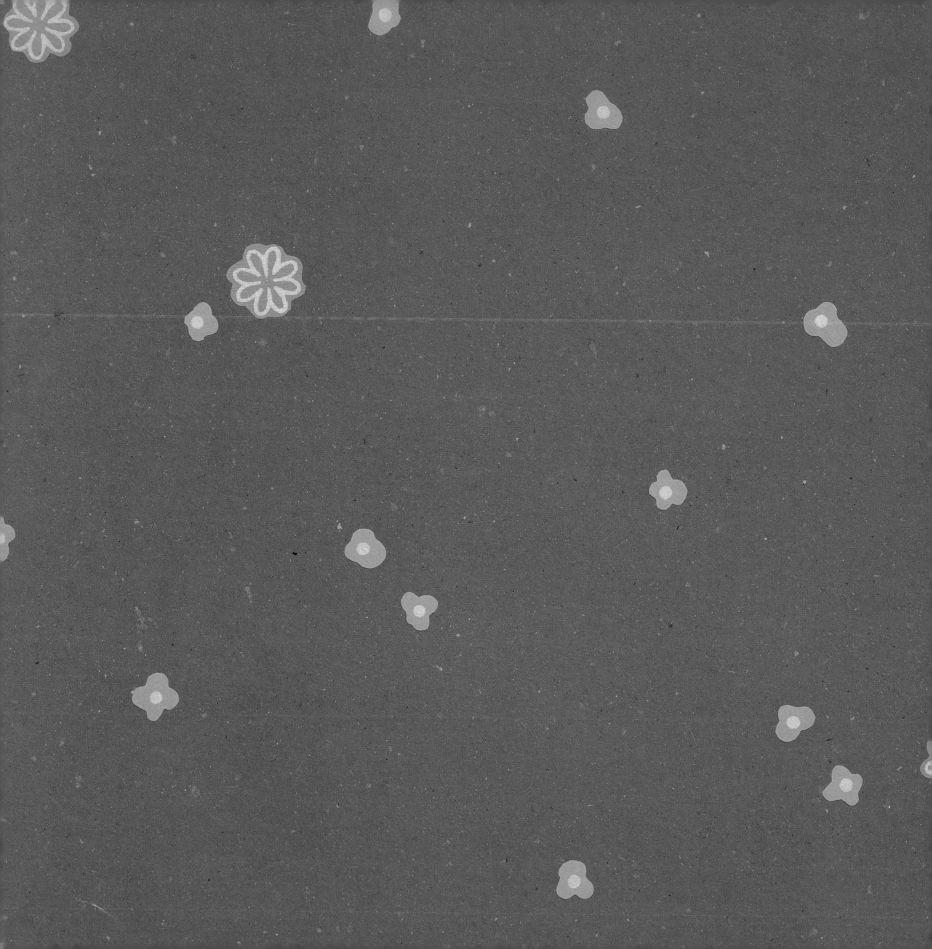

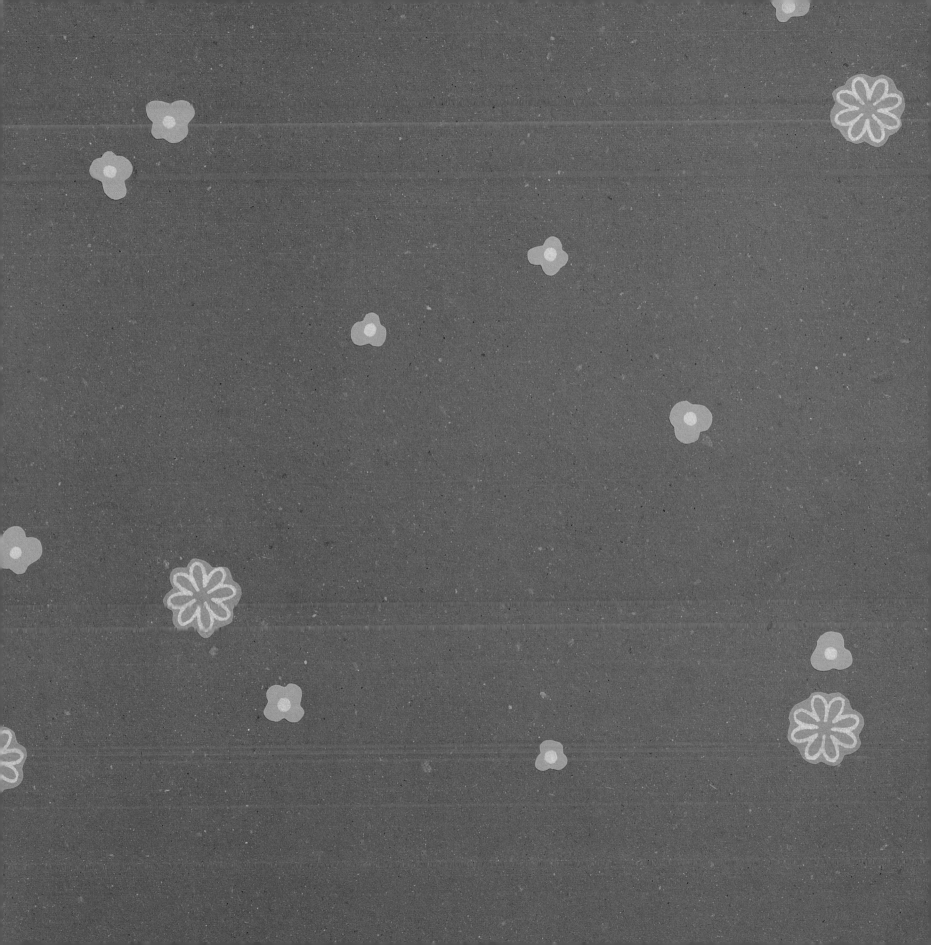